Catch Me, if

Written by Jill Eggleton
Illustrated by Brent Chambers

"Catch me, Cat," said Mouse.

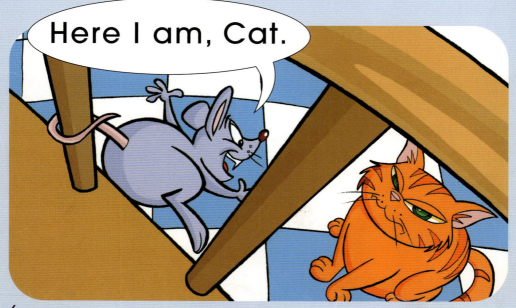

"Catch me, Cat," said Mouse.

"Catch me, Cat," said Mouse.

A Trail

Guide Notes

Title: Catch Me, Cat
Stage: Early (1) – Red

Genre: Fiction
Approach: Guided Reading
Processes: Thinking Critically, Exploring Language, Processing Information
Written and Visual Focus: Trail, Speech Bubbles
Word Count: 118

THINKING CRITICALLY
(sample questions)
- What do you think this story could be about?
- Look at the title and read it to the children.
- Why do you think the cat kept chasing the mouse?
- Why do you think it was easy for the mouse to get away from the cat?
- Why do you think the cat got stuck in the bucket? How do you think the cat will get out of the bucket?

EXPLORING LANGUAGE

Terminology
Title, cover, illustrations, author, illustrator

Vocabulary
Interest words: cat, mouse, cupboard, catch, bucket
High-frequency words: look, at, the, is, in, here, I, am, come, go, me, said
Positional word: in

Print Conventions
Capital letter for sentence beginnings and names (**C**at, **M**ouse), periods, commas, quotation marks, exclamation marks